Sharp Sheep

Vivian French

Illustrated by John Bradley

MACMILLAN CHILDREN'S BOOKS

For all the wonderful children
I've met at the Wordplay Festival, Swansea,
over the past ten years . . . with much love

First published 2005 by Macmillan Children's Books

This edition published 2006 by Macmillan Children's Books
a division of Macmillan Publishers Limited
20 New Wharf Road, London N1 9RR
Basingstoke and Oxford
www.panmacmillan.com

Associated companies throughout the world

ISBN-13: 978-0-330-43989-3
ISBN-10: 0-330-43989-8

Text copyright © Vivian French 2005
Illustrations copyright © John Bradley 2005

A CIP catalogue record for this book is available from
the British Library.

Printed and bound in Great Britain by Mackays of Chatham plc, Kent

Chapter 1

Two loving brothers

Anyone who's got a big brother will know that smiley photos do NOT tell the truth. In fact, you'll probably have guessed that Josh had my arm in an agonizing twist behind my back and was hissing, 'Give it to me!' under his breath. 'Give it to me, or the slippery Slime Monster will come creeeeeeping out from the cupboard in the night and gobble you up . . .'

There isn't a photo to show me handing my new red tractor over in floods of tears. Or sneaking into Josh's room later to steal his RoboCop. Or the fight when he found out, and Mum had to tear us apart. Or how that night I had a terrible nightmare (I used to get a lot of those) and I told Mum it was because Josh had told me about the Slime Monster, and he said I was a slimy sneak and we had another fight.

So you can see that Josh and I have always been typical big brother, little brother, and it didn't change as we got older. He'd push me, I'd shove him. I'd steal his comics (he had a passion for those really gory comics about vampires and skeletons and rattling bones right from when he was about eight) and he'd kick my train tracks up in the air (I had a passion for trains). Sometimes he'd take me to the park to play football, but then he'd put me in goal and shriek with laughter every time I missed the ball. Which I did ninety-nine times out of a hundred. So then I'd draw whiskery moustaches on his football heroes when we got home. (Wayne Rooney looked great. Especially when I added great big boils on his nose and chin.)

More fighting.

Mum would sigh and moan and tell us off, but it didn't make any difference . . . until Josh moved on to secondary school, grew a foot overnight and found out he could beat me up properly. All of a sudden I couldn't get my own back, however hard I tried, and I tried really, really hard . . . but it always ended up in a fight, and he always won, and that was no fun at all. As you can imagine, I was beginning to get totally fed up with him when something we'd never expected in a million years happened. Mum fell in love.

When Mum met Rick, BOOM!!! It was love at first sight. And no, he didn't turn out to be a wicked stepfather. He was a really nice guy, and I should know because he was my form teacher. Actually, I suppose it was me that brought Rick and Mum together, because they met at a parent–teacher evening at the end of term. Rick told Mum how my maths was awful and my sporting skills were nil, and Mum looked into his eyes, and little pink hearts and

flowers danced and fluttered all around them. It was only about three months later when he moved in – and that was fine by me.

Not for Josh, though.

Like I said, Josh and I hadn't been getting on at all well. He seemed to think he was the biggest bestest star of stars ever, and if he took any notice of me at all it was to bash me up, preferably in front of his secondary-school mates. Luckily he was hugely into football, so he was out loads playing up at the park (I was NOT invited) or doing some kind of after-school practice, so we didn't see much of each other. Which was good. And then Rick moved in, and we were forced together. Which was bad. VERY bad.

I'd sort of wondered how Josh would feel about Rick, because Rick was SO not interested in football, but it turned out it wasn't him Josh went on and on and ON about. It was Rick's daughter, Mandy. She came as part of the package, and of course she needed a bedroom. Josh asked Mum why Mandy couldn't live with her mum and just visit Rick for weekends, but Mum wasn't having that at all. Mum said Mandy had lived with Rick ever since she was a baby and her mum had zoomed off to Australia, and she needed to be with her dad. I thought that might have made Josh a bit more sympathetic, because our dad had vanished into the arms of an American woman when I was two, but it didn't. He said he wasn't going to share a room with me even if Martians were going to invade and it was the only space left on earth.

Josh's next bright idea was that Mandy could share with me, but Mum wasn't having that either, much to my relief. Mandy was the year below me at school, and I knew she was a nice kid, but sharing a room with a GIRL? No, thank you.

Mum sat us down and got heavy. She didn't do it often, but when she did even the new super-sized Josh took notice.

'You two will have to share,' Mum told us. Josh growled and gave me a filthy look. 'Tell you what –' Mum sounded as if she was giving us a real treat – 'the two of you can have my room – it's bigger, so you'll have lots of space. Probably more than you've got now, in fact. Rick and I'll have your room, Josh, and Mandy can have Paul's room . . . and we'll all be happy little bunnies!'

I don't know what Mum's idea of a happy bunny was, but from that moment on Josh turned into the grumpiest bunny in the universe. In fact, I reckon the bunnies would have chucked him out of their burrows and left him to the foxes.

Rick helped us move our stuff. He was really nice about it, drawing a chalk line down the middle of the room and telling us funny stories about how he used to share with his kid brother and they'd made their room into a no-go area for adults, with cunning booby traps and tripwires and stuff. Josh didn't say a word.

He looked black as thunder, and the moment Rick had gone he scuffed out the chalk line with his boot.

'This is MY room,' he snarled, and he glowered at me like the black-fanged monster on the cover of his latest comic. 'You can sleep here because you have to, but don't you ever touch ANYTHING of mine!'

And I didn't argue because I knew he'd wipe the floor with me if I did. I went out of the room instead, and for a fraction of a second he looked disappointed . . .

And that was when a big shining light flashed on in my brain. *If Josh wanted to pretend the room was his and his alone, then I'D pretend HE didn't even exist. TA-DA!!!*

Time went on. Things got worse. I just kept quiet, and practised pretending Josh didn't exist, but it wasn't always easy. There was a lot of him, and he made sure he took up all the space he could.

I didn't answer when he yelled at me for moving his tottering heaps of horror comics . . . which I hadn't touched. Well, only just enough so I could find my way into bed. I went downstairs when he started chucking everything round because he couldn't find his homework diary. And when we were both in bed and he tried to tell me gruesome stories from the comics he'd been reading I pretended I was asleep.

Before we shared a room there was a time when I was always pestering him to tell me exactly those sorts of stories – but there's a huge difference between being told about hideous ghouls and ghosts in the warm cosy light of the sitting room, with Mum doing the ironing, and hearing about blood and fangs

9

and scratchy-scratchy claws when it's pitch dark. Before, when Mum was listening with me, Josh's stories sounded nicely creepy, and good fun. It was one of the times when we actually sat in the same room without trying to kill each other. But after we'd moved rooms, and I was in the lower bunk bed surrounded by dark shadows, and Josh's voice was floating

eerily down from above, and the curtains were making a creepy swishing noise, everything changed. To be honest, it freaked me out, but when I asked Josh to stop he wouldn't. He got worse, so I pulled my duvet right over me and put my head under the pillow. That way I couldn't hear anything. I could shut him out as completely as if he was on another planet.

Chapter 2

I haven't said much about Mandy.

She was a little skinny girl with big brown eyes, and she mostly stayed around Rick, or Mum if Rick was out. If they were both out she vanished into her room. She always seemed to be listening for Josh's thumping boots, and at the first click of his key in the front door she'd melt away. At first I couldn't understand why she was so nervous of him, but she must have been picking up on the fact that he blamed her for his losing his room, even though nobody had ever told her so. Even Josh hadn't said anything outright.

Maybe it would have been better if he had.

What he did was to tell her horror stories when we were meant to be doing our homework . . . and I had to listen to them as well, and there was nothing I could do about it.

He told us that the ghost of a little boy haunted our house. Josh said the boy had a scar on his face that dripped real blood as he staggered from room to room.

'Drip . . . drip . . . drip . . .' Josh said in a deep growly voice. 'Drip . . . drip . . . drip. Just listen, Mandy . . . be very still. Can you hear it? Drip . . . drip . . . drip . . .' When Mandy squealed and put her hands over her ears Josh looked dead pleased with himself. He looked even smugger when Mandy wouldn't go to bed that evening on her own.

I knew how she felt. When I woke up about midnight and went to the toilet and heard the sound of dripping I nearly passed out – until I remembered that the bathroom tap always drips. It used to drive me mad when I was in my old room – Mandy's room now. And then I wondered if Josh had been thinking about the tap when he made up the bit about the dripping blood. Was he making up stories to fit the odd little quirks and happenings in our house? When I heard his next story I couldn't help thinking he was.

According to Josh, a wicked old woman had died in Mandy's room long long ago, and no one had found her for months and months. Her blood had soaked into the floorboards and could never be scrubbed out. That, Josh said, was the reason Mandy had the only bedroom with a fitted carpet, a carpet with nails round the edges to stop it ever being taken up. A cold shiver crawled up and down my spine when he said that, because he was quite right about the nails. Judging by the look on Mandy's face she'd noticed them too.

Then Josh told Mandy there was a werewolf with huge long teeth and white foam dribbling from its slavering jaws that lurked in the garden and howled when the moon was full. If it ever bit you, Josh said, you'd grow long bristly fur all over your face and hands, and you'd never be able to sleep again. Part of me was beginning to see how clever he was being, because the night before Vicky-next-door's dog had howled and howled all evening . . . and the moon had been full. Other parts of me didn't feel the same way at all, because I was beginning to have horrific dreams. Also, I couldn't help but see what he was doing to Mandy. I couldn't avoid it, because I was there, every evening, sitting on the other side of the kitchen table.

So why didn't I tell Mum – or Rick – that Josh was scaring Mandy into nightmares every single night? Because I was scared of him, that's why. But I could see Mandy getting paler and paler, and quieter and quieter. There was a thin partition wall between our bedroom and hers, and sometimes I could hear her crying. Especially when Vicky's dog was howling . . . and, if I'm honest, I wasn't happy either. I kept having this nightmare about falling down a big black hole and not being able to climb out because the sides were slippery with bright red blood. Yuck. It was much MUCH worse than the Slime Monster I'd been so scared of when I was little. I'd wake up all sweaty and trembling.

I didn't really understand why Josh was being so mean. It wasn't actually Mandy's fault that we had to all change rooms; if anything, it was Mum's fault for falling in LURVE. And Mandy was OK, for a girl. She was so quiet, you didn't need to notice her if you didn't want to. She didn't fill the place up with Barbie dolls, or nail polish, or whatever girls usually do. When Josh was out with his mates she was always up for a challenge on my Game Boy, or a game of Monopoly, or

whatever. She wasn't bad at football, either –
in fact, she was really quite good. Miles better
than me, although that wasn't difficult. I
didn't tell Josh that, though. Maybe because
football was what he was best at. Most of all
I didn't tell him because if I ever mentioned
Mandy he always got ten times worse.

Mandy herself never said anything about
Josh's stories. The second she could get out of
the kitchen she went away by herself and read.
She liked reading; she had loads of books in
her bedroom.

Chapter 3

Then came the big news. Mum and Rick were having a baby. Mandy cheered up no end, and Rick and Mum looked all glowing and pleased with themselves. Josh went quiet. Ominously quiet. He even stopped telling us stories at homework time. He just sat at the end of the table and glowered, and drew skeletons all over his homework diary in thick black felt tip.

When Mum and Rick came back from the second scan to see if the baby was growing OK, the two of them were waving this weird black-and-white photo as if it was a prize.

'Look!' Mum cooed. 'Just LOOK! You can see it's a boy! You can all help choose his name!'

'Lucifer!' Josh said, and he stormed out of the room slamming the door behind him.

Mum looked startled, and Rick's eyebrows whizzed up, but all he said was, 'Hmm. We'll have to add that to the list. What do you think, Mandy?'

Mandy was gazing at the splodges of black and white as if they were the most beautiful thing she'd ever seen.

'I don't know,' she said slowly. 'It needs to be something really special. Can I think about it?'

Mum gave her a massive hug. 'Lucky baby to have such a lovely big sister,' she said, and Mandy smiled a huge smile I'd never seen before. I suddenly realized she was quite pretty. Usually she looked so pinched and peaky she reminded me of those photos of Victorian orphans – the ones that were forced to work in the coal mines.

'What do you think, Paul?' Mum's voice broke into my thoughts. 'What do you think we should call him?'

I stared at the photocopy of the scan. 'Erm . . .' I said. 'Couldn't we wait and see what he looks like when he pops out?'

Mum laughed. 'Fair enough,' she said. 'He's not due to arrive until the end of the summer holidays, so we've got plenty of time.'

But we hadn't.

The last day of term Mandy and I came struggling back from school carrying all the usual sort of end-of-term junk, and there was Mum waiting for us at the front door. She was looking dead pale, and she was clutching at her enormous stomach.

'Hi, kids,' she said, and she sounded breathless. 'I'm sorry, but I think this baby's on the

20

way. Doesn't feel as if he's going to wait . . .'

My mouth dropped open, and my head whirled. What was I meant to do? I'd vaguely heard jokes about boiling water, but I didn't really have a clue. Mandy said, cool as a cucumber, 'Have you phoned the ambulance?'

Mum nodded. 'It's on the way. And Rick's coming home as fast as he can. But I've phoned Gran, and she's twisted her ankle – and I don't know what to do about you three.'

'We'll be fine,' Mandy said. 'Won't we, Paul?'

'Er . . . yes,' I said.

'You mustn't worry, Sarah,' Mandy went on, 'it's bad for you. You'll soon be back home again with our baby –' Mum smiled at that – 'and we can all help you. It'll be fine!'

Mum started to say something, but she was interrupted by the ambulance roaring up from one direction and Rick tearing up on his bike from the other direction. Then Josh came strolling round the corner with a gang of his secondary-school mates. Everyone – except Mandy – started talking at the same time, but then Mum bent over and made a loud moaning noise, rather like a cow with terrible toothache. Josh's mates vanished, and the ambulance crew swung into action. They bundled Mum on to a kind of chair-stretcher contraption and whisked her into the back of the ambulance, and Rick scrambled in as well. Then the doors were shut, and they zoomed away.

Mandy and I stood looking after them, still holding our end-of-term paintings and clay pots and bags.

Mum's last words echoed in the air . . .

'There's a big pizza in the freezer. Mandy, you're such a sensible girl – I'll leave you in charge until Rick gets back . . .'

Josh suddenly turned round and headed for the house. He stormed through the front door and we could hear the slam of the bedroom door from outside. Mandy and I looked at each other, but we didn't say anything. We went into the kitchen. I turned on the TV, and Mandy got the pizza out.

Rick came back about nine that evening. We heard his key in the lock, and Mandy shot out of the kitchen to meet him.

'Has he come? What's he like?' she asked, dancing round and round him as he came through the door. 'Is he big? Have you chosen a name?'

'Just a minute! Patience, young lady!' But Rick was smiling as he came into the kitchen and slumped on to a chair. 'Hey – where's Josh?'

'I think he's in his . . . our room,' I said. I didn't say we hadn't seen him since Mum left. I'd shouted up the stairs when the pizza was ready, but he'd taken no notice. In the end the two of us had eaten most of it while we watched TV.

'Run up and fetch him,' Rick said to Mandy. 'We don't want him feeling left out.'

Mandy hesitated for a moment, but as she moved towards the door Josh came in.

'Dad's got some news about the baby!' Mandy burst out.

'I'm starving,' Josh said, and headed for the bread-bin.

'Me, too,' Rick said cheerfully. 'Hang on a tick, and then I'll scramble some eggs – but there's something I need to tell you all first.'

Josh propped himself up on the table next to me, and Mandy leant against Rick's legs.

'Well – you've got a new baby brother!' Rick said, and his grin almost split his face in two. 'He arrived in a huge rush, and he weighs five pounds exactly, so he's still very little – and that's where we've got a problem. He needs to stay in the hospital for at least a week while they keep an eye on him, and of course your mum has to be there too . . . but we've sorted it all out. Tomorrow, early, I'm going to drive the three of you to Wales, and Gran and Grampy Jenkins will look after you until your

24

mum and the baby are OK to come home. Oh, and we've decided we won't choose a name for the baby until you get back. Promise.' And he sat back in his chair and grinned and grinned.

There was a long silence. Then Mandy said in a small shaky voice, 'Do we have to?'

Rick nodded, and got up. 'It'll be fine, duckie. Sarah says they're longing to meet you, and Josh and Paul can tell you all about them and Longstepping House on the journey down.'

Josh said, very stiffly, 'I thought Gran had hurt her ankle.'

'She's not great,' Rick said, 'but she's sure she can manage if you all help out. And when she's better she'll come back with you on the train, and stay for a few days so's she can see the new baby and give Sarah a hand.' He winked at Mandy. 'She can teach you how to change nappies . . . and then you can train up Paul and Josh!'

'Where will Gran stay? There's already too many people in this house.' Josh sounded dead grumpy.

'She can share with Mandy.' Rick was determined not to have his happy mood ruined by Josh's scowl. He ruffled Mandy's hair. 'You'll have got to know each other by then, so you won't mind, will you?'

Mandy shook her head. She had her Victorian orphan look on big time.

'And now,' Rick said, 'I'm STARVING! What shall we have, Josh?'

'I'm not hungry,' Josh said, and he went out of the kitchen and thumped up the stairs.

Chapter 4

Rick woke us up really early the next morning, and stood over us while we shoved clothes into Mum's old suitcase and a couple of carrier bags. Mandy had a neat little case of her own, and Rick obviously thought she'd know what she was doing because it was me and Josh that he badgered to hurry up and get on with it. We had a scratchy sort of breakfast (Rick said we'd stop for a proper breakfast halfway there, at a service station) and piled outside and into Mum's old car.

Which wouldn't start.

Rick said a few rude words, which wasn't like him, and we moved on to plan B. There was a flurry of phone calls, Vicky next door gave us a ride to the station, and it suddenly turned out that Josh, Mandy and I were going the whole way by train – on our own.

'Dad . . .' Mandy said as we tramped on to the platform at Bristol Parkway station. She was almost blue, she was so pale, and her voice was trembly. 'Dad – couldn't I stay with you? I PROMISE I won't get in the way!'

Rick tried to do his hair-ruffling thing, but Mandy moved her head away. Rick patted her shoulder instead. 'You'll be fine, duck,' he

28

said. 'These brothers of yours will look after you, and Grampy Jenkins will meet you at Neath station. He says *his* car's working fine!' He gave what was obviously meant to be a jolly cheering-up kind of laugh. 'Here.' He handed Josh two ten-pound notes. 'Make sure you get yourselves something to eat on the way, and you can share out the change for pocket money.'

Ten minutes later we were sitting on a train rumbling towards Wales. Josh and I were sitting together, and Mandy was the other side of the table next to a spindly woman who was knitting. The woman looked as if she'd like to talk to us; she kept giving us little half-smiles, but Mandy had already hidden herself behind the pages of a book, and Josh was staring fiercely out of the window. I could hear him rustling the ten-pound notes in his pocket, and I was wondering what would happen if I suggested we got something to eat. Rick had said the journey would be at least an hour and a half, and I was ravenous. I looked down the corridor to see if the man with the food trolley was coming, but I couldn't see any sign of him. Instead the spindly woman caught my eye.

'Going away on holiday, dear?' she asked brightly.

'Erm . . . yes,' I said.

'That's nice. Where are you off to?'

'Neath,' I said. It wasn't true; Grampy and Gran live at least a good hour's drive away, north-west of Neath and right up at the top of a valley, on the edge of Carmarthenshire, but I didn't want to get into a complicated discussion. I could feel Josh pushing at my ankle.

'Lovely!' The woman smiled. 'And are you going to see your grandma?'

'My brother and I are going to see *our* grandparents,' Josh chipped in. He sounded suspiciously friendly. He pointed at Mandy. 'That little girl there's coming with us because she hasn't got anywhere else to go. Our grandparents are very kind, so they said they didn't mind if she tagged along, even though Gran hasn't been at all well recently.'

I could see Mandy flushing a deep painful pink behind her book, and the woman looked taken aback. I was pretty shocked myself.

'I see,' the woman said rather feebly. 'That's . . . that's very kind of them. Well, I'm sure you'll have a wonderful time.' And she went straight back to her knitting. When we reached the next station she gathered up her things and left, with a little wave at me and a sorrowful smile at Mandy, who didn't look up.

By the time we got past Cardiff almost everyone else had got off, and the three of us were alone. Josh got up and took himself off to the buffet, and came back with three packs of sandwiches and three tins of Coke, which he slung on the table. I seized the cheese and tomato and got stuck in, but Mandy didn't move her eyes from her book.

'Aren't you hungry?' I asked.

She shook her head and went on reading.

When we'd finished eating Josh leant forward. 'Mandy,' he said, 'shall I tell you about Gran and Grampy Jenkins?'

'It's OK,' Mandy said in a very small voice. 'You don't need to bother. I'll find out when I get there.'

'I just thought I'd better warn you,' Josh said, and he tried to wink at me. I ignored him, and he looked put out, but only for a moment. 'You see, it's not like Bristol. It's wild, and bare, and Longstepping House is the only house for miles and miles and miles.'

'There's Longstepping Farm,' I interrupted, 'and the farm cottages –' Josh glared at me.

'The only house,' he went on, 'except for a farmhouse where a mad old farmer lives.'

I thought of saying that Farmer Jordan isn't actually old, or mad, and his wife, Sheila, is great, and their little boy, Tomas, is always coming round and knocking on Grampy's door to see if Gran's been cooking – but I didn't.

 32

'And all around the house are sheep . . . sheep like you've never seen before. They're not white, but brown, because these sheep are special . . . very special. Once, long long ago, they were snow white, but then –' Josh's eyes were positively glittering – 'there was a terrible battle between the devil and the angels. The angels wanted the sheep for themselves, because they were so beautiful, but the devil wanted them too. They had curly horns on their heads, just like he did, and he knew they belonged to him, and he challenged the angels to a tug of war. The angels caught the sheep by their tails, and the devil caught them by the head. At once their heads turned black, and their coats turned dark, but their tails stayed white as snow.

'The angels pulled and pulled, but the devil held on, and at last he won. As he seized the sheep in triumph all their tails turned black as soot . . . but the tips are still white, just to remind you that the angels lost.'

Mandy had put her book down and was staring at Josh with wide eyes, like a rabbit caught in the headlights of a car. I was too. I'd never heard that story before, and my stomach was very chilly . . . even though I was almost sure Josh had been making it up while he was staring out of the train window. Almost, but not quite. Farmer Jordan's sheep really do have white tips to their tails. And brownish coats. And black heads.

'Hey!' I said, suddenly remembering. 'They've got a white stripe on their face as well!' Josh kicked me so hard it hurt, and went on with his story.

'Of course, the devil wanted to make sure the angels never came sneaking back to steal his sheep.' His voice sank to a hoarse whisper, and Mandy leant towards him as if she was terrified of missing a single word. 'He looked around for a shepherd, and in a dark and dirty village he found Rhys, a man who boasted that he'd cut the throats of a thousand men in just one night. The devil offered Rhys a bargain, and Rhys agreed. He would look after the devil's sheep, and in return the devil promised that Rhys would live for ever and ever. And sometimes, when the mists are down on the valley, you can hear Rhys calling to the sheep, and whistling to his invisible dog.

And sometimes a stranger is stupid enough to wander into the valley, and he's found in the morning with his throat cut open and blood oozing out over the grass. But sometimes –' Josh had both me and Mandy hanging on his

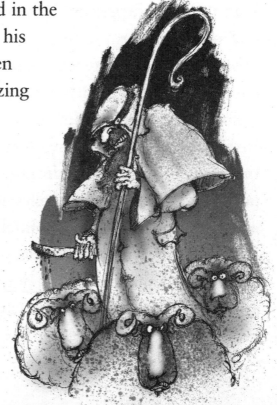

every breath by now – 'people come up to the valley on purpose, because if anyone is brave enough to stay out with the sheep all night and Rhys *doesn't* catch them, then he gives them a wish. A real wish. And that wish will always come true . . . it's the Magic Wish of Rhys the Fleece.'

Josh finished his story and sat back in his seat looking incredibly pleased with himself. I found that I'd forgotten to breathe and had to puff and pant for a moment or two.

Mandy looked at me, her face white as paper. 'Is it true, Paul? Is what Josh says true?'

For a moment I didn't answer. I felt as if Josh had suddenly changed in front of my very eyes into something horrible and poisonous. It made me feel sick, and as if I was being torn in half. I was almost sure the story wasn't true – at least, the bit about Rhys and the magic wish – but my ankle was hurting badly, and I'd probably be sharing a room with Josh at Gran's . . . and I'd

36

definitely be sharing with him for ever when we got home. And I was scared.

'Yes,' I said, 'it's absolutely true.' And even as I said the words I felt as if I'd put my hand on something slimy and dead and rotten, and I wished I could unsay it, but I couldn't.

'And is it true about the wish? Do you promise that it's true?' Her eyes were huge, and I wondered if she could see into the back of my head. I had to look away as I said, 'Yes. I promise.'

Chapter 5

The Balwen Black Mountain sheep has a base colour of black/brown or dark grey, with a white blaze on the face, four white feet and a half-white tail. The name Balwen is derived from the Welsh word Bal, meaning a white blaze. Similar to the South

Wales Welsh Mountain in hardiness, ease of management and good mothering ability.

By the time the train pulled into Neath station I was completely fed up with travelling. And with Josh. Mandy hadn't said another word, but had read until she finished her book, and then gone to sleep. Or pretended to. I do enough pretending myself to know that it's usually pretend sleep if your mouth stays shut and your head doesn't flop. Josh had gone to get more sandwiches and crisps, which he'd eaten all by himself, and then he'd played some weird game on the mobile phone that Rick had lent us in case of emergencies. Occasionally he'd say, 'WOW! Look at that! Top score!' and he'd show me the phone, and before I could see what it was he was showing me he'd snatch it away again.

We heaved ourselves out of the train with our bags and cases . . .

. . . and the hideous sick feeling inside me floated away.

There on the platform was Grampy Jenkins, twinkling and beaming all over – and Gran was there beside him, leaning heavily on a stick. She was waving madly and calling, 'Hello! Hello!' and as soon as she could get hold of us she was hugging me, and telling Josh how he'd grown, and hugging Mandy too.

'So – now we've got a granddaughter to spoil!' she said. 'Isn't that a good thing, with all these boys! You and me and Sarah, we'll have our work cut out keeping them all in order. Now, into the car with you, and we'll be off this minute.'

I'd forgotten how safe Grampy and Gran make me feel. It was like being a little boy again. Josh must have felt the same way, because he was really chatty all the way in the car. I hadn't heard him talk like that for months and months, and I felt better and better and lighter and lighter as each mile rolled by. He was sitting in the front beside Grampy while Gran sat in between me and Mandy in the back, and I heard him telling Grampy that he'd been in the first-year football team at his school and had scored more goals than anyone else. He'd never mentioned that at home.

'Fantastic! We'll have to have you out on the field later, giving us a demo!' Grampy said as he carefully negotiated a sharp corner. The valley road is full of hidden bends and unexpected twists in the road, and there's a steady climb up and up and up that made me very very glad we weren't in Mum's dodgy old car. As usual the roller-coaster drive was making me feel sick, and I stared fixedly out of the car window, leaving Gran to talk to Mandy.

SCREEEEEECH!!! Grampy slammed on the brakes and we skidded to a halt. Gran screamed, Grampy swore and Josh and Mandy gasped. In front of us three sheep were standing right in the middle of the road, chewing steadily, and staring at us with strange yellow eyes. They didn't even flinch as the car stopped inches away from their noses.

I could see that Mandy was frozen in her seat, and I wasn't surprised, because these were the sheep from Josh's story. They were black all over except for the white blaze on their faces, and the white on the end of their tails. Their curly horns glinted in the sunshine, and they never took their eyes off the car.

'For heaven's SAKE!' Grampy said, and he hooted his horn loudly. The sheep took no notice. He hooted again, but it had no effect whatsoever.

'Bloomin' animals,' Grampy muttered. He opened his door and began to get out. The largest sheep let out a loud 'Baaaaa!' and then the other two joined in.

'Baaaaa! Baaaaa! Baaaaa!'

The mournful bleating bounced off the rocks, and echoed to and fro and to and fro until it sounded as if thousands of ghostly sheep were hovering all around us. I saw Josh bite his lip, and Gran shivered. Mandy was paper pale, and I think I was too. As the baaing gradually faded, the three sheep in front of the car nodded at us. Once, twice, three times. Then, with a toss of their heads, they wheeled away and trotted off the road . . . and in seconds they'd completely disappeared.

For a moment or two nobody said anything. Then Grampy got back into the driving seat and slammed the door shut.

'Always been famous for the echo, this valley,' he said as he started the engine. 'Sounded like a sheep's chorus, if you ask me!'

Gran and Josh laughed. Mandy gave a nervous little giggle, and Gran patted her knee.

'Odd things, sheep,' she said. 'Never can tell what they'll be up to next. Now, let's hope we don't get stopped again, or my pie'll be ruined. I've been cooking all morning!'

And off we went.

As we drove away I turned round to look behind me – and there were the three sheep back in the road. Staring at me . . . but this time they were shaking their heads.

'No. No. No, no, no.'

I didn't say anything. My stomach felt as if it was full of freezing-cold stones, and I knew if I tried to speak my voice would tremble.

Chapter 6

Gran really had been cooking all morning. There was a huge meal waiting for us when we finally trailed in the door, and even after all his sandwiches and stuff Josh ate enough for about three people. Mandy didn't eat a lot, but she did begin to look less see-through.

After we'd finished Gran said, 'Now – there's a bit of a turnaround upstairs. I know you and Paul usually share, Josh, but I thought you might like to be the big boy on your own for once. Grampy and I are sleeping in the sitting room just now, because of the bathroom being here on the ground floor – it's easier for me with my ankle, see – so you're in our room. Paul's in the spare room, and we've made up a nice little space for our new girl in Grampy's study. I hope you'll be all right with that.'

 46

All right? You should have seen Josh's face. He was actually whistling as he carried Mum's case up the stairs. He even took my bags up without being asked, while I took Mandy to show her where Grampy's study was. It's a neat little room at the back of the house, next to the kitchen, and it's one of my most favourite rooms ever. It's full of pictures and drawings of flint arrowheads and Stone Age men and humps of grass that Grampy swears are burial mounds (he's an ancient-history fanatic), and one wall is full of books from floor to ceiling. Grampy's table was pushed back, and the camp bed was made up with lots of pillows and Gran's best home-knitted blanket on the top. It looked dead cosy, but as I looked round I realized something was missing. Grampy had removed his collection of chunks of pot and old arrowheads and bits of bone. Usually they were on his table, carefully arranged in a big glass case. There was even a mini collection of ancient human teeth, three

47

of them still in a jawbone; Grampy reckoned they were over a thousand years old, and he was hugely proud of them. Josh and I had been fascinated by them when we were little, but Gran had never been that enthusiastic. She called the collection Grampy's Bone Yard, and made him dust it himself.

'Sarah told us you liked books,' Grampy said as he followed us in, 'so we thought you'd be happy in here. All her old school books are there, see – just help yourself.'

Mandy smiled the huge shining smile that we hardly ever saw. 'Thank you,' she said. 'It's lovely!'

'We'll leave you to settle in,' Grampy said. 'Paul, you can help me with the dishes.'

'I can help with the washing-up!' Mandy said eagerly, but Grampy shook his head. 'We'll spoil you today. It's not every day I get given a pretty granddaughter! We'll set you to work scrubbing all the floors and sorting the peas from the beans tomorrow.' And he gave her a big wink as he hauled me away to the kitchen. As we went he whispered, 'I moved the Bone Yard to the outhouse. Thought it might give the poor child bad dreams!'

We had a great afternoon. Gran said she was going to have a snooze and rest her ankle, and Mandy said she wanted to read, so Grampy took me and Josh for a long walk down the valley and across into Lower Meadow, where the grass was grazed lawn-mower short by the sheep. It was SO like the old days. We took a football with us, and Josh must have been telling the truth about his goal scoring because every time Grampy pointed to a pair of bushes and said, 'Goal mouth!' Josh put the ball exactly in between them. You could tell Grampy was impressed, and that made Josh show off more and more. I was useless, as usual, but that made Grampy and Josh laugh, and Josh gave me a couple of tips about using the side of my foot, not the toe. I tried it out, and actually managed to hit one of the bushes, and he slapped me on the back. It was FUN. As we were walking back, Josh dribbling the ball neatly round the rocks and stones, Grampy was outlining his future career playing for Man United, or Arsenal.

'I suppose I'll have to get used to the idea you'll not be playing for Cardiff City,' he said with a mock sigh. 'It'll be the big league for you, boy, and no mistake.'

'Josh can earn enough to buy us all a great big house,' I said. 'And I'll have a big posh car as well, please!'

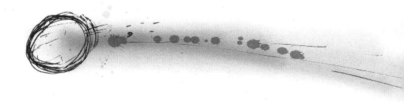

Grampy laughed. 'You and Mandy can be his agents,' he suggested.

'Actually, Mandy's good at football too,' I said, quite without thinking.

And that's how I ruined it.

Josh gave the ball a massive kick, and sent it hurtling off into the distance. Then he stormed after it, and when he caught up with it he booted it again. Even harder. As I looked miserably after him I heard a reproachful 'Baa . . .' from a nearby field.

Grampy looked at me. 'Trouble?' he asked.

I shuffled my feet. 'It's nothing.'

'Hmm.' Grampy tucked my arm comfortably into his. 'Sometimes it's hard when you have so many changes. New dad, new sister, and now a new baby. Poor old Josh.'

We walked back to the house in silence. It was a friendly silence, though. Josh was there already, pulling his shoes off in the hall, and he looked a bit better. There was no sign of Mandy, but we could hear a man's voice talking in the sitting room, and Gran's voice answering. She sounded odd. Upset.

Grampy frowned. 'Visitors, is it?' he said, and opened the sitting-room door. I could see Gran sitting very upright on the sofa, and opposite her was Farmer Jordan looking red in the face and uncomfortable.

'Oh, it's you, Owain.' Grampy turned to us. 'Josh, Paul – run and put the kettle on, there's good boys. Make us a cup of tea, will you?' And then he stepped into the sitting room and closed the door behind him.

Josh and I went to the kitchen.

'What's going on?' I asked as I filled the kettle. 'Did you hear anything?'

Josh bit his thumb. 'I think it's something about the house,' he said. 'I didn't know it wasn't theirs . . . did you?'

'No,' I said slowly. 'At least . . .' I searched my memory. 'Mum once said something about it being a tied cottage, and I didn't know what it meant, so I asked her what it was tied to. She said it wasn't that sort of tied. She said it meant it belonged to the farmer Grampy used to work for, but Grampy and Gran could live in it all their life.'

'Oh,' Josh said, 'that's all right then.' He reached up for the teapot, and then stopped with it in his hands. 'Are you QUITE sure? Only I heard Gran say she was too old to move.'

'That's all I know,' I said, and then we heard the front door bang.

'Sounds like he's gone.' Josh put the teapot on the tray. 'Only four cups then.'

'Five,' I said.

Chapter 7

When we took the tea tray into the sitting room
Grampy was sitting beside Gran on the sofa,
and Mandy was on a little stool on the other
side of the room looking anxious.

'Good boys,' Gran said. 'Nothing like a cup
of tea to put things to right, eh, love?'

'That's right,' Grampy agreed, but his eyes
weren't sparkly like they usually were. 'Maybe
Mandy would be mother and pour it out for
us.'

Mandy got up uncertainly, and went over to
the tray. 'You'll have to tell me how you like
your tea,' she said.

'Just milk, precious,' Gran said. 'And the
same for Grampy.'

Josh and I sat down on the edge of the two
armchairs and watched Mandy carefully

pouring out the tea. For a moment there was one of those awkward silences that you get in a place where no one knows anyone else, and everyone is waiting for somebody to break the ice.

Grampy suddenly shook his head.

'It's as bleak as a morgue in here,' he said, and the twinkle came back into his eyes. 'But we're not done for yet. Carys, I'm going to tell these children what's going on. They're not silly, and Paul and Josh will be wondering why Owain never stopped to give them the time of day.'

Gran nodded. 'You go right ahead, love,' she said.

'Just a minute!' Grampy leapt to his feet. 'CAKE! I can't have a serious conversation without cake!' And he zoomed off and came striding back from the kitchen with a plate heaped with slices of rich currant cake.

'That's better,' he said, and he handed Gran a huge slice of cake and tucked her rug round her knees. 'Now, here's the thing. Our cottage belongs in a way to the farm –'

'A tied cottage,' I said, just to be clever.

Grampy gave me what Gran calls his old-fashioned look. 'Be careful you're not so sharp you cut yourself, Paul Thomson. Now, as I was saying, we've got rights to this cottage because I worked with Owain's father as farm manager for thirty years, and if the farm stays in the same hands then there's no arguing with that. But if the owner decides to sell the farm, then everything changes . . . and we'd be asked to leave. And it's been looking for some time as if that could just happen. We've been fighting it, of course, and most of the village is against it, but there are a few who think it could be a good idea . . .'

Grampy stopped for a second and he and Gran looked at each other, and I could see that they were really really worried. 'Still –' Grampy waved his cup in the air – 'we don't know anything for certain as yet, so we won't be downhearted. We'll raise our cups of tea and wish ourselves well instead!'

Josh kept his cup on its saucer. 'But WHY does Farmer Jordan want to sell?' he asked. 'Where's he going?'

'It's not Owain Jordan who's selling,' Grampy said, and he sighed. 'He's a tenant, just the same as we are. He'll have to go too, him and Sheila and little Tomas. That's what he came to talk about. The owner's George Griffith, up in the big house, and he's an old man now, and he's needing looking after . . . and some local businessman has made him an offer. Not sure we know who, do we, Carys?'

'Brand, his name is,' Gran said, and her voice was grim. 'Caradoc Brand, and he should know better. Always a greedy little boy he was, and now – IF he can get the permission from the council – he's wanting to turn Rhys's Field into a great big holiday-caravan site. He thinks he'll make himself a mint of money, Owain was telling me. Pure greed it is, no doubt about it. But he can't do anything without that planning permission.'

'Can't we stop him?' Josh had a fierce expression on his face. 'Couldn't we tie ourselves to a tree? I've seen people on the telly doing that.'

Grampy put his head back and roared with laughter. 'And how many trees do we have up here in the valley, Josh? It would have to be one of those skinny little birch trees, and they'd have you and the tree up in a twinkling!' He went on chuckling, and Gran was smiling too.

'Maybe they'll find an ancient burial mound,' I said. 'One of your stone circles, Grampy. They couldn't build then, could they?'

'They certainly couldn't,' Grampy said. 'And it's an idea that I had too, young Paul. The trouble is, I've been over every inch of that field, and there's nothing there. Only the sheep.'

Gran shook her head.

'That's quite enough about our troubles,' she said. 'Poor Mandy. She'll think she's come into a family with no luck at all.' She glanced across the room at Mandy and tutted loudly. 'Look at the precious girl! She's as pale as pale can be. Don't you worry, love. We'll be fine, whatever happens. Now, who's for a game of Monopoly?'

As Grampy bustled about clearing up the tea things, and Gran got out the Monopoly board, I wondered if Josh had seen how Mandy had flinched when Grampy mentioned Rhys's Field. Had Josh known there was a field up here called that? I didn't know, and I didn't think I'd ask.

Chapter 8

Tomas came knocking at the door early the next morning. We were still eating breakfast, but he came hopping in like a robin hoping for crumbs. He's really tiny for a five-year-old, but he's very independent, and he always comes over if he hears Josh and I are visiting. Usually he gazes at Josh as if he was something really special and follows him round hoping Josh will talk to him, but Gran introduced him to Mandy, and it was weird. Tomas didn't even give Josh a second glance. It was as if he and Mandy had known each other all their lives; within seconds Tomas was sitting on a chair beside her telling her about how his dad's dog had had puppies and how he wanted to keep one for his very own.

'Mam said yes at first,' he said, 'but now she says she doesn't know, and it all depends, but she won't tell me what that means. Do you think that's fair? I don't. I've seen the puppy I want, and I  want to teach him to be like Patch, and look after the sheep. I'm going to be a farmer like Dada when I grow up, and a farmer must have a dog, mustn't he?'

Mandy smiled at Tomas. 'I think he probably should,' she said, 'but sometimes it's difficult having a dog.' She sighed. 'My gran had a dog, but it had to be put down.'

'Was it very old?' Tomas asked.

Mandy nodded. 'He was nearly eleven.'

Tomas put his hand on her arm. 'I know,' he

said, 'you can come and see my puppies. Then you won't be sad about your gran's dog.' He looked at Gran and Grampy. 'Can Mandy come and see them now?'

'Just as long as your mam isn't too busy,' Gran said.

'I don't think she's busy,' Tomas said. 'She's writing lots of letters. I heard her tell Dada that she's going to try and stop us being 'victed. What's 'victed mean?'

Grampy and Gran both spoke at once. Gran said, 'If your mam's writing letters maybe it's not a good time to see the puppies,' and Grampy said, 'Why don't we all go outside for a game of football?'

'YES!' Josh leapt to his feet, but Tomas took Mandy's hand. 'Mum won't mind,' he said. 'Come on.'

'Tell you what, Paul,' Grampy said, 'you go with Mandy. Then you can show her the way back. Is that all right, Tomas? Can Paul come to see the puppies as well?'

Tomas studied me with his head on one side. 'OK,' he said, and then he looked round at Josh. 'You're grown up,' he said accusingly. 'You've got big.'

Josh made a face at him. 'I'm a MONSTER!' he growled, 'a real big MONSTER!'

That always used to make Tomas squeal with laughter and pretend to run away, but this time he didn't. It was odd. His face changed, and for a moment I thought he was going to cry, but instead he frowned.

'You're being a nasty monster,' he said. 'I like NICE monsters.'

We all trooped outside, even Gran. She said she wanted to watch Josh and Grampy playing football, and Josh looked pleased. Tomas, Mandy and I went round the back of the house to the wicket gate that leads out to the field, and as we reached the gate Mandy froze. Standing on the other side was a large dark brown sheep with a black head and tail and curly horns. On its face was a white stripe, and the lower half of its tail was snow white. It was so EXACTLY like the largest sheep we'd seen in the middle of the road that my stomach gave a sudden lurch. When it saw Tomas opening the gate it gave a deep 'Baaaaa!' and stepped towards us. Mandy backed away, but Tomas dragged her forward.

'It's only Harrison,' he said. 'He lived in our kitchen when he was a baby, and he still keeps on trying to get back inside. Don't you, Harrison?' And he gave the sheep's head a friendly rub.

Mandy put out a tentative hand, but Harrison ignored her.

'Baa,' said Harrison, and he was looking straight at me. 'Baaaaa!'

'Hello, Harrison,' I said. I was trying to be offhand and cheerful, but I could understand Mandy's hesitation. There was something about Harrison's pale yellow eyes and black slit pupils that was really weird. I had a horrid feeling that he could see right through to the

back of my brain, and didn't think much of it.

I don't know why people talk about sheep being silly. They always look to me as if they know a whole lot more than us humans and are secretly despising us. When they all get together in the corner of a field I bet they're telling each other stories about stupid human behaviour.

There were other dark brown sheep like Harrison in the field, and as we walked across they raised their heads and stared.

'Josh said the sheep here looked different,' Mandy said, 'but I thought he might have been making it up until I saw those sheep in the road. And these ones. All the English sheep I've seen have been white. Or sort of dirty yellow.'

'These are Balwen Welsh Mountain sheep,' Tomas said proudly. 'My Dada and my Grandada and my Great-Grandada have always had this sort of sheep, and I will too. And when I'm a great big grown-up boy my little boy will keep them.' He stuck out his chest and marched along in front of us as if he already owned the biggest herd of sheep in the world. Harrison trotted beside him, and Tomas put his arm over his back in a proprietorial hug.

Mandy glanced at me over Tomas's head, but I pretended not to see. My mind was full of all kinds of things: Gran and Grampy losing their house, and Tomas all unknowing that he might have his future taken away – and fragments of Josh's story floating in and out like a tune that you want to forget but can't.

'What's this field called?'

I looked at Mandy in surprise. She didn't sound anxious. Just interested.

'This is Rhys's Field.' Tomas always loved being asked questions about his farm. He waved his arm down the valley. 'It goes all the way down to the bottom of the slope. And that's Lower Meadow at the end.' He giggled. 'It's ever so easy to remember. The others are Middle Field and Fat Field.' He gave Harrison a squeeze. 'Harrison likes Fat Field, don't you? The grass is very good, so the sheep get nice and fat. But mostly the sheep go up on the mountain, beyond our farm.'

'Is that your farm over there?' Mandy asked. She sounded OK, but it was such a fantastically warm and sunny day it would have been difficult for anyone to have believed in anything dark and nasty like Rhys the Fleece.

Tomas nodded. The faint sheep path led in a zigzag across the field from Grampy's house to an old stone wall, and then round the wall to an iron gate. Beyond the gate was a clutter of ancient stone buildings, and as we turned the corner we could see Tomas's mother hanging out the washing on the drying green.

We had to climb over the gate to keep Harrison from following us; he baaed plaintively as we jumped down the other side.

'Mam!' Tomas ran to his mother and pulled at her skirt. 'Mam! I've brought Paul and his new sister to see the puppies!'

'That's nice,' Mrs Jordan told him. There were grey shadows under her eyes, but she kissed us and said she was pleased to see us. 'Owain was sorry he didn't say hello when he called round yesterday,' she said, 'but he's got a lot on his mind just now. We've had to sort out a mountain of paperwork, and he can't be doing with that.' She gave us a tired smile. 'It's exciting about your new baby brother, isn't it? We've got babies here too, but ours are up on their feet already!' and she showed us into the back scullery where a black-and-white collie was lying in a basket. Four round fat puppies were tumbling about on the floor beside her, and Tomas bent down and scooped up one for Mandy and another for me.

We stayed and played with the puppies for a long time. They were still wobbly on their feet, but they wanted to explore everywhere and everything, and they thought Tomas and Mandy and I were the most exciting things they'd ever seen. Tomas showed us the puppy he wanted to keep; he said he was going to call it Flyer because the white markings on its back looked like wings.

'An angel dog,' Mandy said.

'H'mph!' Farmer Jordan heard what she said as he came in through the open door. 'More like little devils, those pups. They've

already chewed my boots and knocked over a bucket of slops this morning! Paul, your Grampy's here – says it's time you were getting back.'

Mandy and I got up unwillingly and left Tomas sitting in the basket with the mother dog, his puppy cuddled in his arms.

'Bye,' Mandy said. 'See you again soon!'

Grampy was waiting outside. He asked us if we'd had fun with the puppies, but it sounded as if it was an effort for him to be cheerful.

'No news, then,' Farmer Jordan said. It was a statement rather than a question.

'No.' Grampy sighed. 'I've been in touch with everyone I can think of, but they all say the same. We could put in a bid to buy the land ourselves, but we both know we can't afford that. We can only hope he doesn't get the planning permission, but –' Grampy sighed again – 'it seems he's got friends on the committee. And there's already property up here, so it sets a precedent, apparently . . . and he's a cunning man. He's claiming it'll bring good jobs and trade into the area.'

'What? A lot of holidaying tourists stamping about and scaring my sheep? What trade will that bring?' Farmer Jordan's eyebrows were bristling.

'They won't be your sheep any more, Owain,' Grampy said gently.

Farmer Jordan stood stock still, then turned on his heel and marched away. Grampy watched him go.

'It's his whole life,' he said, 'being here. His family has farmed this place for hundreds of years. He wanted Tomas to follow in his foot-steps . . . but it's looking like that just can't happen.'

'And you'll lose your house too,' Mandy said as we negotiated our way round Harrison and the gate. Grampy hooshed the sheep out of the way with his stick, and Harrison glared at us reproachfully.

'Maybe. Let's keep hoping, though. Maybe

Harrison's a sheep fairy, and he'll grant us a wish.'

Mandy rubbed her cheek thoughtfully. 'Do you believe in wishes, Grampy?' she asked.

Grampy looked serious as he said, 'Do you know, I do. I'm a Welshman, and all Welshmen believe in wishes. You never know how they might come true, though, so you have to be careful what you wish for.' Then he laughed and said, 'And I believe in a good big plate of eggs and chips when it's lunchtime, so hurry yourselves up and we'll be back just in time.' And he grabbed Mandy's hand and began to jog back across the field. I followed on behind them . . . and Harrison followed behind me. And gradually the other sheep fell in line behind Harrison, so it must have looked to anyone watching as if I was playing follow-my-leader – except for one thing: follow-my-leader's a game, and this didn't feel like a game at all. I could feel hundreds of slitted yellow eyes fixed on the back of my skull.

Chapter 9

We messed about for the rest of the afternoon. Josh asked if I'd come out and play football, but I wanted to get out the old Hornby train set that Gran keeps in the hall cupboard. It belonged to Grampy and his brother when they were young, and there was a whole load of metal track and three fantastic trains. Mandy said she'd help me, and Josh glowered at us both before stomping outside. The day before must have been a truce rather than a change in our relationship. He'd been very quiet over lunch, and I had the feeling that his asking me to play football was a challenge. I also had a feeling I might have to pay for turning him down, but the sun was still shining and at that moment I didn't care. If I'm truly honest, I preferred playing with Mandy. She never slapped me down, or argued,

or insisted that she always had first go at everything. And she never ever twisted my ears or
pulled the hair at the back of my neck.

Not long afterwards Tomas came back, and
the three of us set up the track so that it ran
right round the edge of the sitting room. The
trains were great; you wound them up with a
key, and they had two little rods at the back
that you pulled or pushed to make the trains go
forwards or backwards. We built a tottering
hill of books, and the trains just managed to
make it up and over with a load of carriages
behind them and then rumble down to where
Mandy was in charge of the points. We found
Grampy's ancient set of farm animals as
well, and Tomas arranged the sheep and the
horses and the pigs in fields. It was fun, and
it was obvious that Mandy enjoyed it too.
She was laughing, and she chatted non-stop;
I'd never seen her like that before.

'Look!' Tomas said as one train rushed down
the hill and another laboriously crawled up the

other side. 'They're coming up our valley to our farm!' He plonked a sheep on the top. 'There's Harrison! He's watching out to see everything's all right. He does that a lot; he told me.'

'Let's make another hill,' I said. 'Then we can have a valley in between.'

'And here's Gran and Grampy's house!' Mandy waved a station house in the air.

'Where's my farm?' Tomas wanted to know, and Mandy searched in the cardboard box until she found a barn. 'Here,' she said.

'And we can put the sheep in Rhys's Field,' Tomas said, and he began to rearrange his flock.

Mandy moved the second track over to the other side of the valley. 'Who was Rhys?' she asked.

Tomas shook his head. 'I never did meet him. Dada said he was a shepherd, long ago. Dada said he wasn't a nice man.' He held out a sheep for Mandy to put on her side of the valley. Then, out of the blue, he asked, 'What IS 'viction, Mandy? Nobody said yesterday.'

Mandy looked at me, and I didn't know what to say, so I shrugged.

'It's . . . I think maybe you'd better ask your mam,' she said.

Tomas gazed at her, his blue eyes big as saucers. 'It's a bad thing, isn't it? My Mam keeps on crying. And my Dada does too. He thinks I don't see, but I do.'

'Don't worry,' Mandy said soothingly. 'I'm sure it'll be all right.'

Tomas picked up a sheep and held it tightly. 'It HAS to be all right,' he said fiercely. 'It's my Dada's farm, and it's going to be mine. And nobody did ought to make my Mam cry. I HATE them.' And his face went very red and there were angry tears in his eyes.

Mandy put her arm round his shoulders. I'm not good when little kids cry, so I started up one of the trains, and then Josh crashed in through the door.

'Gran says tea in five minutes,' he said. 'And you're having tea here too, Tomas.'

Tomas glanced up at him. 'Look, Josh,' he said, 'we've made the trains come up our valley. There's our farm and there's this house, and there's Harrison in Rhys's Field.'

Josh stiffened. 'Has Mandy been telling you about Rhys's wish?' he asked. He sounded deeply suspicious.

Tomas looked blank. 'What wish?'

'Oh . . . er . . . nothing.' Josh was definitely relieved. 'Five minutes, mind!' And he disappeared again.

Tomas was thinking about what Josh had said. He pulled at Mandy's arm. 'What wish, Mandy?'

Mandy flushed very pink. 'It's nothing, Tomas. Just a silly story.'

'Tell me, Mandy. PLEASE tell me!' Tomas's face was suddenly alight with excitement. I remembered Grampy saying that all Welshmen believed in wishes.

'Well . . .' Mandy hesitated. 'Shall I tell him, Paul?'

'Don't ask me,' I said. Actually I thought it was a daft idea, because Tomas gets obsessed about things, and turns into a total monster if he can't get what he wants . . . but then again, Mandy was a girl, and she probably knew what she was doing.

'There's a story,' Mandy said slowly, 'that if anyone stays out all night in Rhys's Field then they can have a wish. But it's only a kind of folk tale.'

Tomas jumped up. 'But that's EASY! We can go and get a wish easy-peasy lemon squeezy, and then my Mam and Dada'll be happy again!'

'No –' Mandy tried to catch Tomas, but he danced out of reach. 'It's not like that, Tomas. It's . . . it's got to be misty. And it's dangerous.

78

Rhys was a bad, bad man . . . why, even your dad told you. And he might catch you!'

Tomas came to stand close beside her, his eyes sparkling. 'I'm not scared of bad men,' he said. 'I'll MAKE Rhys give me a wish! You can help me. I know – you and Paul can come too!'

'Oh, Tomas,' Mandy said unhappily as she looked at his hopeful face, 'forget about it. It's only a story. I shouldn't have told you. It's – it's a secret story.'

Tomas put his finger on his lips. 'I'm GOOD at secrets,' he whispered. 'I won't tell ANYONE!'

'That's good,' Mandy said. 'You're a very good boy. Now, promise me you'll forget all about it –'

I thought maybe I could distract Tomas. 'Come and have some tea,' I said, and I got up and went into the kitchen. I could hear Tomas whispering urgently in the sitting room behind me, but Gran was talking to me and I couldn't go back.

Chapter 10

All through tea Tomas kept smiling a happy conspiratorial smile at Mandy. She looked flustered and embarrassed, especially when she saw Josh staring at her. He stared at me too, and he hardly spoke at all. Gran and Grampy were unusually quiet, and it wasn't a comfortable kind of meal.

Farmer Jordan arrived for Tomas soon after we'd finished, and Gran asked me and Mandy and Josh if we'd mind doing the washing-up.

'Grampy's got to go to a meeting in the village tonight,' she said, 'so he's walking back with Owain and they'll go down the valley together.'

Mandy and Gran cleared the table while Josh ran the hot water into the sink. He had a strange expression on his face, a mixture of cunning and delight, and my heart sank.

'You can leave all this to us, Gran,' he said. 'You go and sit down.'

'That's kind of you, Josh,' Gran said. 'I must admit to being a bit tired.' She sighed. 'It's all this business about the house, I expect. It'll be a relief when we know one way or the other, although I've no idea what we'll do if that Caradoc Brand man gets his way.' And she limped off to the sitting room.

Josh closed the kitchen door, and his eyes were gleaming as he plunged the dishes into the sink.

'Have you told Mandy,' he said as he sloshed hot water round and round, 'that there's a terrible story about this house?'

'No,' I said gruffly and picked up a handful of dripping forks. I began to dry them unnecessarily thoroughly.

'But Mum told us,' Josh said, and he sounded so genuine and innocent that I stopped my polishing. 'Don't you remember? She told us ages ago. It gave you nightmares it was so terrible. So she never told us again.'

I shook my head, but a vague memory of Mum telling us about when she lived here floated into my consciousness. Her stories were mostly about when she was growing up, and the people living in the village below. But nightmares? I didn't know. I'd had so many nightmares when I was little . . .

'But you haven't heard the story, have you, Mandy?' Josh's voice was soft, but it made me nervous.

Mandy shook her head and began wiping a saucepan with her back to us.

'Well,' Josh began, 'you must have noticed that this is a very old house. There have been Thomsons here for hundreds of years, just like Tomas's family at Longstepping Farm. It's always been a happy house up until now, but there's a curse hanging over it. A terrible curse that will mean that Thomsons no longer live here. It came about because one of the first people who lived here had a wife who was a white witch. She could cure sick sheep, and she could make apple trees have extra apples, and do all kinds of good things. The only trouble was that she didn't want any strange women, or girls, coming to her house, just in case they were bad witches and spoilt her magic, so she made a spell. The spell protected everyone who lived here just as long as they respected her wish. The Thomson men could bring their wives here, and it was all right if they had daughters, but no strange girls must ever stay longer than three nights . . . or the curse would fall, and the Thomsons would be driven away.' Josh slapped the last plate on to the draining board so hard that it cracked in two. He looked taken aback for a second, but then he nodded at the two pieces of china.

'You see? You've been here for one night. And tonight will be the second . . . and already things are starting to go terribly wrong. Of course, Gran and Grampy are much too kind to say anything. They don't like the curse ever to be mentioned – in fact, they'd be very cross if they knew I'd told you. They'd say there was no such story. But they must be worrying about it. Don't you think so, Paul?'

I didn't answer. I was looking at him, wondering what he was trying to do. Also, something was niggling at the back of my mind, but I couldn't work out what it was.

Josh picked up a tea towel and flicked it at me. 'I said, don't you think they'll be worrying about the curse?'

I was saved from answering by Gran opening the door.

'Finished already?' she said. 'That's good!'

'I'm really sorry, Gran, but Mandy broke a plate.' Josh patted Mandy's shoulder as if he was comforting her. She moved sharply away, and her face was blank. I couldn't tell what she was thinking.

Gran dropped the two pieces of plate in the bin. 'That plate's been mended so often it's time it went for good,' she said. 'And it's a

 84

good sign. Out with the old, and in with something better.' And she nodded at Mandy as if Mandy had done something wonderful. Mandy gave Gran her wonderful sun-coming-out smile, and Josh scowled.

'Now, we've got time for a game of cards, if you want to play,' Gran said as we stepped over the railway tracks and moved into the sitting room. She went over to the window to draw the curtains. 'It's getting very misty out there. I hope your Grampy won't be too late back. What would you like to play?'

Josh wanted to play racing demon, but Mandy said she'd rather read, if that was all right. I saw Gran give her a thoughtful look, but she just said, 'Of course you can, precious,' and began dealing out the cards.

Grampy still wasn't back by the time we went to bed. Gran kept saying she wasn't worried, and he'd probably gone to the pub with Farmer Jordan, but I saw her peer out of the window quite a few times while we were going in and out of the bathroom and getting ourselves settled.

When Gran came in to say goodnight to me she had another look out of my window.

'He'll be fine, Gran,' I said. 'He knows his way with his eyes shut.'

Gran nodded. 'I know he does. No . . . it was the sheep I was looking at. What do you think they're doing? They've been there all evening.'

I hopped out of bed and joined her at the window. Outside I could see the fence between us and Rhys's Field. And it was weird. Two sheep were standing side by side, their noses almost touching the barbed wire. They weren't moving. They were just standing.

'They look as if they're waiting for something,' Gran said. 'Silly things! What can they be thinking of?'

'Tomas says his pet sheep, Harrison, talks to him,' I said as I climbed back under my duvet.

'That boy!' Gran smiled as she tucked me in. 'Although he might be right, at that. Tomas is a little Welsh Mountain boy through and through.'

'Grampy's a Welshman,' I said. 'Can he understand sheep?'

Gran grinned at me. 'Your Grampy's like me – he's from Cardiff, so I think he's more likely to understand buses!' She gave me a kiss. 'Don't be too long reading, now!' And she limped away through the door.

I was just about to switch my light off when I realized I needed to have a pee, which was dead annoying because you have to go all the way downstairs in Gran's house. I slid out of bed and trotted off along the passage and down the stairs. I was just shutting the bathroom door when I heard Grampy come back. There was a rustling, which I guessed was him hanging his coat on the hooks in the hall. And then I heard Gran come to meet him, and I suddenly felt awkward. I didn't know if I should make a noise to let them know I was there . . . and it seemed easier to keep quiet, so I did.

'How did it go, love?' Gran asked.

Grampy made a gloomy harrumphing noise. 'Not good,' he said. 'There's a man coming up from the council tomorrow morning to look at the projected site, as they call it. And it sounds as if our Mr Brand is coming with him to show him his plans.'

'Oh dear,' Gran said.

'And it gets worse,' Grampy went on. 'Apparently he's already talking about putting a site manager in our house and turning Owain's milking sheds into a top-quality toilet block with hot showers.'

'And what about the farm itself?' Gran asked. Grampy gave a disgusted snort.

'Converted into holiday cottages,' he said. 'Ten separate units, with car-parking space in the yard.'

Gran gave a long heavy sigh. 'It makes it seem so real when you describe it like that,' she said. 'Whatever will we do?'

I was beginning to feel terrible. I was sure they'd never have said as much if they'd known I was listening. Luckily for me, Gran said something about a cup of tea and they went into the kitchen and shut the door. I zoomed upstairs, and back into bed, but it took me ages to get to sleep. I don't think I'd properly realized before that the whole world of the farm and the fields and Gran and Grampy's house was under such a huge threat; it was like a massive black cloud looming over the sun, taking the colour away from everything. Longstepping Farm and Longstepping House had been part of my life for ever . . . it felt as if someone had knocked on my door and said, 'Hello, young man – we're about to take your leg away!'

Chapter 11

I woke up with a start from a peculiar dream about sheep jumping through hoops. But something very real was making a noise loud enough to wake me up. I lay rigid, listening.

'Baa.' From outside came a familiar mournful bleat. And then another. 'Baaaaa!'

And suddenly something cracked open inside my head, and a muddled collection of things people had said that day tumbled out, and I knew what had bothered me about Josh's story.

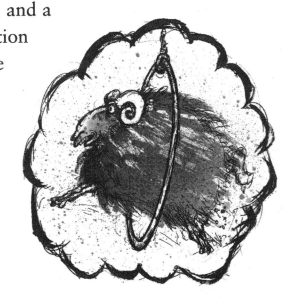

The sound of the sheep made me think of Tomas and his farm . . . and Grampy saying Tomas's family had lived at Longstepping for hundreds of years.

And that made me think of Josh saying there'd been Thomsons – OUR family – here for hundreds of years as well . . .

BUT if Grampy Jenkins came from Cardiff, that couldn't be right. I had the answer now! Grampy had said he'd been here for thirty years . . . ONLY thirty years!

I sat up. Josh's story about the curse on Longstepping House was made up. It wasn't something Mum had told him at all. He'd made it up on purpose to scare Mandy . . . again.

I got slowly out of bed and went to the window. There must have been moonlight beyond the mist, because I could make out the sheep quite clearly. The stripes on their faces were shining white, and a faint gleam showed the curl of their horns. They hadn't moved since the last time I'd looked, except that now they were staring up at my window.

'Baaaaa!'

And then I saw something else. A small figure in jeans and a sweater had one hand on the gate. In her other hand she was holding a torch with a thin, watery beam. The light was wavering and shaking wildly, as if she was terrified, but as I watched she lifted up the metal latch.

You can never know just how much I wished I hadn't seen Mandy. I wanted more than anything else on earth to jump back into bed and pull the covers over my head . . . but I didn't, even though my stomach felt as if it had a bucketful of frozen worms in it.

I was going to have to make a decision. Do something. But what?

Should I rush after her? And where was she going anyway? Was she running away because of Josh's stupid story about a girl bringing bad luck to Gran and Grampy? My mouth went dry. Was this why Josh had kept on telling her stories? To make her run away?

Or had she believed the story about Rhys's magic wish? Was Mandy truly brave enough to go out into Rhys's Field in the mist . . . and was she going to stay there all night long?

I swallowed hard and watched as Mandy pushed her way past the two sheep. One gave a last loud accusing 'Baaaaa!' and then turned to follow her as she walked unsteadily away. The other sheep stayed where it had been all evening, but looking up at me. Staring. It was willing me to do something.

I stood and dithered, and while I was dithering Mandy was swallowed up by the mist. I leant my head against the cold hard glass of the window. I HAD to do something – but what? If I woke up Gran and Grampy, what would they think? No. It had to be something else – and I knew, as my mind whirled round and round, that I was trying desperately to avoid facing up to the obvious.

I had to get Josh, and we had to find Mandy, and somehow I had to make Josh tell her his stories weren't true . . . and make her come back.

As I crept across the landing my heart was beating like a tom-tom. I could actually feel it whanging against the inside of my chest. Every step, and every creak of the floorboards, was making it beat harder. As I put my hand on the door handle I wondered if, after all, I should just go on my own . . . I could tell Mandy Josh had been making it all up, couldn't I? That would be much much easier . . . for me. But what would happen when we got back here again? Josh would just make up another story, and everything would go on . . . and on . . . and on. And it would be horrible.

I stared at the closed door. All I had to do was turn the handle . . . but my hand wouldn't obey my brain.

Then the door opened. Wide. My heart leapt into my throat.

 94

'Paul?' Josh was glaring at me. 'What the hell are you doing? I thought it was a burglar creeping about!'

I made a strangled noise, and then gulped. 'It's Mandy,' I managed at last. 'She's gone out into the field, and we've got to get her back . . .' My voice trailed away.

Josh snorted. 'Why?'

'Because we DO,' I said, and I knew as I spoke that I was sounding pathetic. 'Gran and Grampy would be furious if they knew you'd . . . that is, if they knew she was looking for a wish. We have to tell her it was a lie, Josh . . .'

Josh didn't answer. Outside, the moon must have pushed through the mist, because I could see his face, but it was impossible to tell what he was thinking. Or feeling. At last he said, 'If she wants to go chasing about in Rhys's Field, that's her lookout. I'm going back to bed.' And he closed the door in my face.

I could feel the frozen worms in my stomach

knotting up, and there was a hard cold lump of something in my chest, something that was growing heavier by the second . . . and then an extraordinary thing happened. I realized I was angry. How DARE Josh shut the door on me? Then a huge earth-shattering thought came shooting into my brain like a skyrocket. Wasn't that what *I* did? I, Paul Thomson, was ALWAYS shutting doors . . . not literally, but shutting things out. Things I didn't like. Putting my head under the pillow. Pretending the bad things weren't there. Hoping they'd go away all by themselves. Not telling. Not saying. Not answering.

And if I didn't do something about it now, I never ever would.

I took a huge breath, and opened Josh's door.

'JOSH,' I said, 'Josh, you've GOT to come and help find Mandy. We've GOT to go and tell her to come back. And if you don't tell her your stories are great big fat horrible lies, I'll . . .' I gulped. 'I swear I'll wake up Gran and Grampy,

 96

and I don't care any more what you do . . . I just
don't CARE!'

Then I turned, my hands sweaty and my heart
thumping, and I tiptoed down the stairs. At the
bottom I remembered I'd forgotten to bring any
shoes with me, but I didn't go back. I held my
breath as I passed the sitting-room door, and
heard the steady 'Umph . . . Umph . . .' of
Grampy, and the 'Ssss . . . Ssss . . .' of Gran.

Chapter 12

The back door was on the latch. I stepped cautiously out into the dark misty night, and the cold wet grass made my toes curl. I shivered – and had an inspired thought. For years there'd been a heap of old wellington boots in the outhouse, left over from various rain-soaked holidays. I trod carefully to the door and heaved it open. It took a moment for my eyes to get used to the gloom, but then – result! I pulled on the first two I found and was about to leave when the shine of glass caught my eye.

A glass cabinet was balanced precariously on a pile of flowerpots behind the boots. Grampy's Bone Yard! I could see the faint gleam of white bone behind the glass . . . ancient white human jawbone . . .

and a wild idea zipped into my head. I didn't stop to think it through – there wasn't time.

I flumped out in my too-big welly boots with my pyjama pocket bulging. I didn't know what had happened to me; it felt as if I had woken up to find I was an entirely different Paul Thomson. Very probably a Paul Thomson who was going to get himself into trouble. BIG trouble. Or was I in some weird and peculiarly vivid dream? For the moment, I didn't care. *I* was going to *do* something.

There was the sound of heavy breathing, and a 'Baa!' from the sheep by the fence. I walked as steadily as I could to the back gate, and I knew it was watching my every step. As I opened the gate it began to move, and I froze, but it wasn't coming towards me. It looked at me hard, then walked steadily away. I just knew it wanted me to follow it, and everything was feeling so unreal that I did. I never thought to look behind to see if anything was following me.

The mist had lifted a little, and I could see further . . . but not far enough to tell if there were any lights on at Longstepping Farm on the other side of the field. Then I realized the sheep wasn't heading that way. It had turned and was moving steadily down into the valley, where the field sloped sharply, and the mist was thicker. I hesitated, crossing my arms across my chest. It was a warm night, but the floating fingers of fog were cold and damp.

'Tomas!'

It was a very faint cry, but I knew it was Mandy's voice. It came from the darkness below, and as I listened I saw the sheep peer over its shoulder as if to check I'd heard her call. I stumbled into the longer grass and followed my guide as it moved on and on ahead of me. The white tip of its tail was like a marker, and easy to see even as we walked down into the gloom.

'Tomas!' The cry came again, and this time there was an answering wail. The sheep began to move faster, and I hurried after it as fast as I could.

'Mandy?' I shouted into the mist. 'Mandy, where are you?'

And then I slipped, and I half rolled and half scrambled down a steep and stony slope . . . and arrived at the bottom bruised and battered and scratched. I flung out my hands to catch at something to stop myself falling any further, and my hands clutched thick curled wool.

'Baa! Baa! Baaaaa!'

I was in the middle of what felt like thousands of sheep. As I staggered to my feet they began to push at me with their hard bony heads. I panicked, but as I flailed about in the sea of horns and solid fleecy bodies I was relentlessly pushed further and further forward.

'Mandy!' I yelled. 'Mandy! Are you there?'

And suddenly I was in open ground, the sheep behind me, and the pale beam of a torch wobbling in my face. I heard Mandy say, 'Oh, PAUL! Thank goodness you're here! It's Tomas – I've found him, but he won't come home, and I don't know what to do!'

Tomas began to wail again. I moved towards Mandy, and she clutched at my hand and shone the torch down on Tomas, who was lying curled up on the ground. He was shivering, and he had a scratch under his ear that was oozing blood. I squatted down beside him, and felt in my pocket for my hanky.

My pocket was empty. No hanky . . . and no jawbone. I had a flash of panic; where had it gone? It must have fallen out . . .

But at that moment nothing mattered except Tomas.

'Don't worry,' I said, trying to sound brave. 'Mandy and I'll take you home.'

Tomas gave a little moan. 'No,' he wailed. 'No! I WON'T go home! Got to see Rhys . . . I've got to have a wish for my Mam and my Dada . . .'

And at exactly that moment a tall black figure in a long flowing cape came stepping towards us out of the mist.

Tomas screamed, 'RHYS!'

103

I couldn't breathe.

Mandy said, 'JOSH?'

And Josh saw the blood on Tomas's neck glistening red in the light of the torch, and he fainted.

If Josh hadn't got in first I think I'd have fainted myself. I'll never forget the way he loomed out of the mist, the moonlight behind turning him into a black silhouette. But when he fainted, and Mandy and I bent anxiously over him, he was definitely a thirteen-year-old boy. A boy wearing Grampy's old mac, and Grampy's hat that was slipping sideways off his head.

He came round almost at once, but then he was terribly sick.

'I'm sorry,' he kept saying. 'I'm sorry.' And then he was sick again. 'It's the blood,' he said as he wiped his mouth for the second time. 'I . . . it makes me feel so sick . . .'

As Mandy went back to Tomas, Josh crawled up to sit beside me. He glanced over my shoulder and gave a watery smile.

'Look!' he said, and he took Mandy's torch and swung it round.

I had to smile too. We were surrounded by a circle of sheep, with Harrison in the middle.

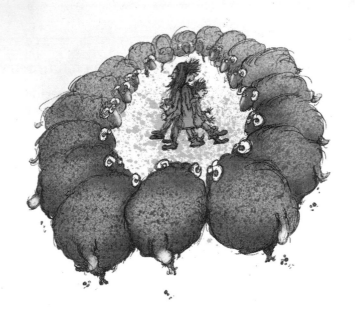

All of them were nodding their heads up and down. Up and down. Up and down.

Tomas struggled on to Mandy's lap. 'I want to go home now,' he said. 'I've seen Rhys, so Mam and Dada will be OK. We won't be 'victed no more.' And then he leant his head on Mandy's chest and began to cry.

I don't know what made me suggest that we put Tomas on Harrison's back, but it worked. Tomas stopped crying, and smiled as he held on tightly to the thick fleece. And of course

106

Harrison knew exactly which way to go. Mandy and I walked one on either side of him, with Josh behind, and as Harrison carried Tomas steadily back up the hill Mandy told me how Tomas had decided he was going to get a wish that night, whether the mist came down or not.

'I tried and tried to make him promise he wouldn't go looking for wishes, but he just wouldn't listen,' she said. 'He was so determined he could save everything. So of course I had to creep out and try and stop him . . .

107

but there was a big sheep – I think it was Harrison – and it kept getting in the way and headbutting me until I went the way it wanted me to go. It brought me down here to where he'd fallen. I'd only just found him when you arrived.'

'And Josh,' I said.

'Yes.' There was a long silence, and then Mandy said, 'Why did he come?'

'Ask him,' I said, and I looked back at Josh trudging behind us. 'Josh! Mandy wants to ask you something!'

'What?' Josh took a couple of quick steps to catch us up. 'What did you say?'

Mandy hesitated, and then said, 'I just wondered why you were here.'

'Paul told me to come.' Josh said, and there was a curious note of – could it have been respect? – in his voice. 'He said it was all my fault.' There was another silence, then, 'They weren't really true, you know. My stories. I made them up.'

 108

'Shh,' Mandy said quickly, and she pointed to where Tomas was drooping on Harrison's broad back. 'He thinks he's got his wish . . .'

Tomas shifted and said in an anxious voice, 'I do have my wish, don't I, Mandy?'

'Of course you do,' Mandy told him.

As we reached the flat part of Rhys's Field, the mist rolled away and the moon shone out brightly. Harrison quickened his pace as he headed for the farm. As we finally reached the gate a light snapped on in a top window, immediately followed by other lights, and then there came the sound of voices calling.

'MAM!' Tomas shouted, 'MAM, I'm here!'

'Tomas! Tomas?' Mrs Jordan flung open the back door, Josh heaved the gate open, and our curious looking cavalcade trotted through. As Mrs Jordan lifted Tomas into her arms Harrison gave a loud and self-satisfied 'Baaaaa!'

It wasn't the right time for explanations. Mum would have had sixteen purple fits if

109

she'd found us wandering about in the middle of the night, but Mrs Jordan was so desperate to get Tomas washed and cleaned and safely tucked into bed that she didn't seem to notice anything odd about it. Farmer Jordan appeared in a pair of stripy pyjamas and stood rubbing his eyes, but all he said was, 'Little fellow been sleepwalking again? It's too much for him, all this business with the farm. You three get off home to bed, and we'll see you in the morning.'

Chapter 13

We walked slowly back across Rhys's Field. The moon was shining so brightly Mandy didn't need her torch; you could see every tussock of grass and clump of thistles. My oversized boots had rubbed one heel raw and I was limping, and Josh didn't look too good either. Even in the moonlight he looked green.

I noticed Mandy was frowning, and then she said, 'I still don't understand why Josh is here. I thought he hated me.' It was almost as if she was talking to herself.

It was hard to tell for certain, but I think Josh blushed. 'Paul said you believed what I told you. He said you were going to get a wish . . . or running away . . .'

Mandy stopped dead and stared at him. Then she looked at me.

'Did you really think that?' She sounded shocked. Really shocked.

I nodded. And because we were there in the middle of the night, and the moonlight made everything unreal, and there was part of me that couldn't believe any of it was happening, I said, 'I knew you were scared by Josh's stories. I used to hear you crying at night.' And to make her feel better, I said, 'I was scared too.'

'Sorry,' Josh said.

Mandy's eyes opened very wide. She gave herself a kind of shake and said, 'Yes. I was crying. But I wasn't SCARED. I was MISER-ABLE!' Her voice began to rise. 'Don't you see? Don't you understand anything? Didn't you ever think about what had happened to me? You'd stolen my dad! It used to be just me and him, and it was GREAT! And then suddenly – BAM!!!! I'm stuck in your horrible house and I knew you didn't want me and there was nobody I could talk to, because Dad was always mooning over your mum – and I HATED EVERY MINUTE!' She was shouting now. Josh and I stood and gaped. It's true. Our mouths were hanging wide open.

'I didn't mind . . .' I began.

Mandy turned on me and she was trembling, she was so furious. 'You did! You DID! You were only nice to me when Josh wasn't around. At least he was ALWAYS nasty! Your mum was the only one who made me feel she wanted me . . . but I kept thinking it was pretend because she wanted Dad to be happy. But then they said about the baby, and I thought things might just be OK after all . . . but we got sent away here . . . and your POOR Gran and Grampy are going to get dragged out of their house just like I was dragged out of mine . . .' and she threw herself on to the moon-silvered grass and cried and cried and cried.

I'd never known anyone cry like that. Josh and I stood, one either side of her, and didn't know what to do. And we looked at each other, and I knew he was feeling just as bad as I was. And I wished so much that Mum was there, and I got a terrible prickling feeling at the back of my throat, and my eyes were wet, and I desperately needed a hanky . . .

'Baaaaa!'

It was Harrison.

'BAAAAA!' He was standing right behind us, and if ever a sheep looked puzzled, Harrison was that sheep.

And Mandy sat up, and she looked at Harrison, and began to smile . . . and then she looked at me and Josh. I guess we must have looked like kids at school who know they've gone too far. WAY too far.

'You look just like Harrison,' she said, and giggled.

Josh grinned back. 'He's got more sense,' he said, and then he added, 'Why didn't you tell Gran about Tomas?'

Mandy made the kind of tsking noise that

114

people make when someone's REALLY stupid. 'Because I'd have had to tell her about the stories, of course,' she said.

'Oh.' Josh put his hands in Grampy's mac pocket. 'Er . . . thanks.'

Mandy got to her feet. 'That's OK,' she said.

'Baaaaa!' Harrison said, and he headbutted Josh so hard that if I hadn't been in the way he'd have gone flying . . . and Mandy totally cracked up laughing. The three of us were still smiling as we tiptoed through the back door.

Chapter 14

It was gone eleven before I even opened my eyes the next morning. The sun was streaming in through the window, and I lay back on my pillow just enjoying being awake. Something had changed between Josh and me and Mandy, and it felt good.

As I staggered down to the bathroom in my pyjamas I met Josh coming up the stairs yawning his head off.

'You'd better get out of those before Gran sees you,' he said, and when I looked down I saw what he meant. My PJs were covered in muddy smears and grass stains.

I shot into the bathroom and zoomed back upstairs to get dressed. I hid my PJs in my backpack, but I needn't have bothered. When I went down to the kitchen Gran was sitting eating toast and marmalade with Mandy, and Mrs Jordan was on the other side of the table.

'Hello,' I said, and I dithered in the doorway.

'Come and have some breakfast,' Gran said, and she twinkled at me, so I knew she wasn't cross. 'I hear you were all out on a midnight walk last night!'

'Erm . . . yes,' I said. I was conscious of Mandy looking at me meaningfully. 'It was a lovely night,' I added, and wished I hadn't, because it sounded so feeble. Gran didn't seem to notice, luckily.

'Hi!' It was Josh, and he hesitated at the door just as I had.

Gran laughed. 'It's all right, Josh. I've been hearing all about your midnight walk! And I'm glad it turned out so well . . . who knows what might have happened to Tomas if you hadn't seen him coming out of the farm gate?'

Josh made a noise that might have been a cough as he sat down. 'Yes,' he said, and I saw

Mandy give him a tiny nod of encouragement. 'Well . . . it was just lucky.'

Mrs Jordan shook her head. 'He's always had nightmares and dreams,' she said, 'but nothing like last night. He's been telling us all sorts about a big black figure, and Rhys from the field giving him a wish – it's unbelievable what his little mind comes up with.'

I couldn't look at Josh, or Mandy.

'Where's Grampy?' I asked. 'Is he outside?'

There was a sudden electric buzz in the air.

'He's out in the field with Caradoc Brand,' Gran said. 'The planning officer's there, and so is Owain. They're waiting for the police.'

'The POLICE???'

Josh and I nearly fell off our chairs.

Mrs Jordan leant forward. She was lit up with excitement. 'You'll never guess what's happened,' she said. 'That Brand man found a jawbone down under the birch trees! And the planning officer says it's a human jaw, and he's called the police! Your Grampy says it's

118

old, but it doesn't make any difference. The police still have to investigate. And Caradoc Brand is huffing and puffing because Owain says it'll mean police digging to look for more bones . . . and the planning man says no way can he allow permission for new buildings until it's all cleared up, and it could be months before that happens.'

'WOW!' Josh's eyes were shining. 'Gran, can I go and see?' And he whizzed off without waiting for her answer.

'So . . .' I said slowly. I wanted to be clear about what was happening, but I also didn't want anyone to look too closely at my face. 'So does this mean there won't be any sale after all?'

'We can't say that,' Gran said. 'But from what's going on outside, it sounds as if Mr Brand might be having second thoughts. Serious second thoughts!'

'Good,' I said, and helped myself to toast. As I stretched for the butter I caught Mandy's eye, and she smiled her best ever sunshine smile.

'There's some more news as well,' she said. 'Dad phoned, and your mum's coming home with the baby the day after tomorrow.'

'And if Grampy's all right with the idea, I'll come back with you on the train,' Gran said. 'I can't wait to see the new boy!' She patted Mandy's hand. 'Maybe a girl for us next time, eh, Mandy?'

Mandy grinned. 'Boys are all right,' she said. 'Most of the time.'

And that's it, really. The police arrived, and they stamped about a lot, and they took the jawbone away. To begin with they were a bit offhand, and Caradoc Brand tried hard to make them say it would be OK to go ahead with his plans. But then they found some human teeth, quite a long way away from the jawbone, and they got really excited, and said the whole field would have to be searched.

Caradoc Brand deflated like a balloon, and

slumped off to his big shiny car and drove away. Grampy had a call later from the estate owner, Mr Griffith, to say he wasn't going to sell; the offer had been withdrawn. Also, he'd been thinking maybe selling wasn't such a good idea; his sister had decided to come and look after him, and she had a huge family . . .

Oh, and just as we were leaving the house with all our cases and bags, Tomas came flying up to the house, his face bright red with excitement.

'Dada says I can have my puppy!' he yelled. 'And I'm going to call him Flyer and we're going to look after the sheep better than anyone ever did!'

And you won't be surprised to know that at once there was a loud 'Baaaaa!' and there were Harrison and his cronies with their noses up against the gate. I couldn't help wondering who, exactly, would be looking after who . . .

Chapter 15

Gran came back with us to Bristol, and we found Mum already at home with a red-faced squalling baby on her knee.

'He does cry a lot,' she said apologetically.

'Can I hold him?' Mandy asked, her face alight.

Mum handed him over and he went on shrieking. Mandy rocked him to and fro, and he stopped for a second, peered at her and then yelled again.

'He's GORGEOUS,' Mandy sighed as she handed him back.

'We haven't got a name for him yet,' Mum said. 'Have you thought of anything?'

Josh shook his head. So did I. Mandy looked thoughtful. 'What about Thomas?' she said. 'Like little Tomas in Wales, but spelled differently.'

'Thomas Thomson,' Mum said. 'Sounds great!'

'Fantastic,' said Rick, and they beamed at Mandy and Thomas Thomson, who was going purple in the face and quivering with rage.

'Oi!' Josh said. 'Oi! Stop that! You'll never be any good at football if you yell at people like that!' And he leant forward and picked the baby out of Mum's arms . . . and Thomas Thomson was completely silent.

'Hi, little bruv,' Josh said.
Very quietly.

For a second I felt weird.
Left out.

Mandy reached across
and pulled my ear.

'Hello, big bruv!' she
said.

And I said, 'Hi, sis!'

Dear Paul,
I thought you might like to know that my Bone Yard collection is going to be famous. After all the investigations they took the jawbones they found in Rhys's Field away, and they're going to be a big feature in the village museum. I asked if they'd like my bits and pieces as well, and they were delighted. Gran and I were very surprised to hear they'd found a second jawbone. I expect you will be too!
Fond love to you all, and come and stay again soon.
Grampy. xxxx

My Family